THE
SERVITOR OF SIN

THE HELLBORN KING SAGA

A fantasy novella by
CHRISTOPHER
G. BRENNING

The Forlorn Sea
Rej Rhivoth
Teb River
Rit
The Hinterwood
Skaginlef
Siln River
Mot
Blackwolf Pass
Borjifa
The Bymist
Pelg
Khorrtal
Brimnora
Morden
Hok
Kepdon
The Plainhold
Dellhaven
Mor Seveht
The Great Sea
Greenwood Forest
Aret
Naxonnos
Cardale
Larssa
Bentmont
Vhos River
Willowsgrove
Corinope
Glimmergulf
Sothfort
Sommerwood River
The Everblue
CALDAKAS

ACKNOWLEDGMENTS

I'T'S DIFFICULT FOR ME TO BELIEVE THIS IS MY THIRD BOOK published in two years. *The Hellborn King Saga* started out as just a crazy idea. I would never have imagined the series would grow to such an extent and develop such an amazing audience worldwide, and I want to personally thank each of you who have been on this journey alongside me.

I want to thank my beta readers, Christopher Jackson and Cheryl Timm, who have helped me since the beginning. Truly, this series would not be what it is without their amazing feedback. I cannot thank you enough for the valuable time you have spent helping me.

I also want to thank all my great friends and fans on Twitter, as well as the awesome reviewers I have come to know, including (but definitely not limited to): Blaise Ancona (Under the Radar SFF Books), Andrew Mattocks (Andrew's Wizardly Reads), Steve Talks Books, and many more. I apologize I cannot list everyone, but I know who you are, and I appreciate every one of you.

And lastly, I want to thank the amazing people in my life, including my mother, Karen. Her support and encouragement has meant the world to me, and has seen me through good times and bad. Also, my great friend Thomas Hunter. Our adventures are worthy of their own book, and may there be many more adventures to come. Cheers, my friend.

I hope you enjoy *The Servitor of Sin*, the prequel to *The Hellborn King Saga*!

for all I have suffered…
for all I have endured…
my fire still burns…

CONTENTS

PROLOGUE

Before the Saga

"HE'S LATE," TOLLAS NORAL GRUMBLED, HIS HORSE STIRRING beneath him. "Far too late."

Negotiations were always a tense affair, especially when Northmen were involved. But nearly two hours had passed since the rider was expected back.

"Likely dead by now," Kavran Martis said, his face grim. He was a dutiful Sergeant, a man of thirty years, and not one for optimism. "Come, Captain, let's get out of here."

"We mustn't lose faith just yet." Tollas sat higher in his saddle, trying to remain stoic.

Behind him stood an army of ten thousand, their massive formation a blight against a dying horizon. At its head was the King himself, Marcellus Bethard of Betanthia. His House's blue and silver colors flew prominently in the distance, its eagle sigil appearing at flight. At first, the men could hardly believe the King had arrived, though his presence only worsened Tollas' anxiety. To fail a Bethard was to court one's death, after all.

A swift gale blew in, rustling a grove of firs on the hilltop. Even the trees, it seemed, were resentful of their presence. Borjifa was an old land, home to ancient people and even older gods. He felt ill-favored eyes watching, studying, and likely conspiring against them. Whether they belonged to trees, birds, or Northmen, their gaze was unsettling.

Tollas removed his steel helmet and peeled away sweaty locks of brown hair from his brow. He saw despair building in the eyes of his standard-bearers, either from fear of the barbarians or of failing King Marcellus. It was difficult to tell which.

"Steady, men," Tollas said reassuringly. "Betanthia's finest are behind us. Commander Valens has bested these savages all his life."

Tollas reflected on his Commander's steadfastness. Cedric Valens was a man of many battles and had come to know the barbarian tribes well. The Bane of the North, some called him, and it was a name most fitting. But even Commander Valens' presence did little to stifle the fear in his men's hearts.

A wicked gust howled and wailed its arrival, gnawing through his thick woolen cloak. Tollas drew his collar tight, stealing away as much warmth as he could. But despite the comfort of an autumn sun, the creeping chill from beyond Betanthia's borders made him shiver. However, it was expected of a Captain to remain unshaken even in the most insufferable of conditions.

He hoped a stony resolve would inspire confidence in his men, for what little it was worth. Yet, despite their overwhelming numbers, facing a northern tribe was anything but straightforward. Fantastic stories often spread throughout their camp, stories that, if not quashed, might impregnate every man's heart with abject terror.

"Northmen are giants, standing ten feet tall! They eat the flesh of those they slay and wear their bones as armor!" a wide-eyed soldier once said, much to his amusement.

The saber on Tollas' hip had spilled enough barbarian blood to know better. They were equally as mortal as the lowliest Betanthian and dispatched just as quickly. Recalling such absurd boasts brought a hint of a smirk to his face, the first amusement he felt in weeks.

Suddenly, the horses around him stirred, some whinnying in agitation. Tollas looked around frantically, hoping to discover the source of the disturbance. He spied a rider at a gallop, a Betanthian, his eyes wide and face turned pale.

"Well, would you look at that?" Kavran snorted. "About damn time he showed up."

The rider came to a halt, struggling to find breath. He appeared unharmed physically, though his spirit was undoubtedly wavering. Tollas cocked his head, dumbfounded at the possibility of such a small tribe defying the might of King Marcellus Bethard.

"They're coming!" the rider announced, then wheeled about.

At first, Tollas expected an attack to follow, given the typical northern disposition. But within moments, he saw an entourage of four men riding toward him, each nearly taller than their horses. Borjifans, they were.

Tollas recognized their chieftain, his gray, bushy hair laden with braids and beads. A crimson cape lay draped across his shoulders, the fabric rustling like a windblown sail. Beside him rode companions of the shield, weathered men who had seen more battles than there were stars in the heavens. Perhaps they had come to swear fealty, Tollas supposed, but Kavran's pessimism appeared to have rubbed off on him.

"Steady, men," he cautioned. "Be on the lookout for treachery. These barbarians are tricksters at heart."

The four riders came to a halt, looking as sour as spoiled meat. But their appearance mattered little. Despite their rabid protests, the village elders had come to treat and hopefully sue for peace. It was the only option in the face of Betanthian supremacy.

"Chief Sanbaen, this is most unexpected." Tollas lifted his chin. "You've come to accept our offer in person, yes?"

A burning fury in the chieftain's eyes was hot enough to melt steel. He spat, disgusted. "Dogs receive a better offer of scraps from your dinner table, Betanthian," Sanbaen grunted. "Your offer is an insult."

"You will not receive a better one," Tollas cautioned. "It would be wise to accept my King's generosity while it remains ripe for the taking. He will not make you another offer."

"We require more time," Sanbaen said, his words tinged with subtle desperation. "We have met your demands on every occasion. Our people have been driven to the very edge of our borders. Where would you have us go? Would you have us pushed into the sea?"

A fifth rider appeared, a hulking beast of a man, bald and bearded. An icy chill crept down Tollas' back, the mere sight of the seven-foot barbarian enough to invite fear into his heart.

"Damien, I told you to stay at the village," Sanbaen snarled at the menacing man.

"I will not sit idle while the last of our birthright is stripped away," the bald barbarian shot back. "These are our lands! Our gods live here! And you would tuck tail and flee once again?"

Dissension among the Northmen was always welcome, but something about the exchange seemed troubling. Tollas felt his hand drifting down to the saber on his hip.

"You have spoken your piece; now hold your tongue," Sanbaen commanded. "Return to the village. We will discuss this matter in private."

"This cannot be allowed to stand," Damien protested. "By the gods, we must—"

"Get moving, savage," Tollas interjected, perhaps unwisely. "These negotiations are above your station. Now act accordingly."

Damien cast a fiery glare, his black eyes both piercing and haunting. Something about the man commanded dread; that much was certain. Thankfully, the massive barbarian took his leave and galloped back to Borjifa without further protest.

"Now," Tollas continued, "I will say this once, and once only. You have until morning to agree and comply. King Marcellus will accept nothing less."

Sanbaen shook his head. "May Zifnir grant you wisdom to turn back from this path. Your hunger for conquest will be the death of this world."

And with that, the Northmen retired, a hissing gale announcing their departure. Tollas was finally able to breathe, a deep exhale escaping his chest. His men looked every bit as relieved as well, though now they would have to report back to Commander Valens. Better the Northmen should have attacked, Tollas thought, than to face Lord Cedric's wrath.

"Come," he said, wheeling his horse about. "We best be heading back."

"Are you certain that's wise?" Kavran quipped, knowing the tongue-lashing that awaited.

Grumbling, Tollas snapped the reins and took off at speed, his riders in close pursuit. Thankfully, their camp lay only a short distance ahead. Torchlight flickered off the tips of sharpened stakes, hundreds, near thousands of them sunk deep into the ground. Sound precautions, he thought, but little more than an annoyance for determined Northmen. Tollas passed through a pair of open gates and by teams of archers standing guard on a crude parapet.

Despite the threat of war, the Betanthian camp was alive with revelry. Soldiers sat around roaring pit fires, hoping to stave off the frigid bite of autumn. Meat and ale were in plentiful supply, as was music plucked from the strings of lutes. One might think it more of a carnival and less of a potential battlefield.

While some officers expressed reservations about such laxity, to Tollas, it was essential to keep morale high. Distractions were often the best antidote for fear, he supposed, fear which might otherwise cripple their army. Soldiers and camp followers greeted him along the way with hoisted mugs and hearty cheers, respect well-earned from dues paid in combat.

A command tent sat just ahead, ringed with burning braziers. Nearly a dozen Royal Guardsmen stood vigil, their ornate breastplates gleaming with rippling orange and red light. Thick purple cloaks adorned their mighty shoulders, a declaration of savage loyalty to House Bethard.

"I don't envy you," Kavran said. "The only thing sharper than barbarian steel is Lord Valens' tongue."

"Perhaps," Tollas snorted. "But nothing compares to the wicked tongue of that wife of yours."

Together they shared their first genuine laugh in what felt like years. Such moments of levity while on campaign were rare, so rare it was a miracle either man even knew how to laugh anymore.

"Indeed!" Kavran smiled. "My Isabelle is quite the fiery one! But the only thing more wicked than her tongue is my appetite. When I return home, I plan on making another son. Tell me, how fares your sister?"

"Lilian is well, though she still mourns our mother's death. Life has been hard for her, but she remains strong. It'll be good to be in her company again soon. But we must stay focused on the task before us. Get some rest, old friend. Who knows what tomorrow might bring? I need you sharp."

"As you wish, Captain." Kavran nodded. "I'll stay close. Someone might need to pry Lord Valens' boot from your ass once he's finished."

With a smirk, Kavran departed, likely headed to one of the many ale carts throughout camp. When Tollas entered the command tent, a thick cloud of incense stung his eyes. He blinked hard, then whisked away a teary droplet. Around a square table stood Commander Valens and several of his confidants, along with Commandant Rupert Denison, head of the northern army. In their hands were glasses of wine, their fingers laden with golden rings.

"Captain Noral," Cedric Valens announced dryly. "What news do you bring from our negotiations? Do those barbarian swine accept the King's offer?"

A rumbling in Tollas' bowels betrayed his resolve. Breaking ill news to the Commander was nearly as deadly as challenging a Northman to a duel. Every man inside the tent stared back with the same indifference, having come to expect the answer.

"No," he responded. "Sanbaen begs for more time, coward that he is. I told him he has until morning to accept our terms, or accept the sword instead."

Cedric ground his teeth, despite his experience with northern stubbornness. "Very well, Captain. Your efforts are applauded. Come, have some wine. We were about to toast our coming victory."

Celebrating before battle seemed foolish, but Tollas was in no position to protest. It seemed wise for a man with higher ambitions to appease those in superior positions. He took up a silver chalice, nearly overflowing with a rustic southern vintage.

There was much to be said about the finer things in life. But on the eve of what could be the biggest battle of his military career, Tollas was anything but cheerful. As he sipped and savored the wine, thoughts of home began creeping into his mind.

"Something troubles you, Captain?" Commandant Denison lifted his chin. He was tall, lean, and distinguished, with a head of blonde hair thicker than sheep's wool.

Tollas was hardly aware of the twisting and tightening his face had undergone, soiling his typically stony composure. "No, Sir. It's just that… even in victory, good men will die tomorrow. Wives will lose their husbands, and children will lose their fathers. Seems inappropriate to celebrate their demise."

A hostile silence befell the tent. The most powerful men in Betanthia looked at him as if he were a traitor to the cause for expressing such thoughts.

"Your sentiment is appreciated, Captain," Rupert Denison said. "Indeed, good men will give their lives tomorrow for a cause greater than themselves. The glory of Betanthia is eternal, is it not? And when we have civilized Caldakas from east to west, north to south, there will come a day when soldiers and bloodshed are no longer necessary. These lands will be at peace. And that, good Captain, is a future worth fighting for."

Suddenly, the men inside the tent snapped to attention. Tollas turned and saw King Marcellus Bethard standing mere feet away, clad in fine linens and thick furs. His brown, shoulder-length hair was loose, a golden band sitting atop his head. It was the most surreal moment of his life, to stand in the presence of royalty.

Tollas remained motionless, too frightened to draw breath. But instinct quickly prevailed, his body rigid and eyes staring forward. Beside the King stood a pair of Royal Guardsmen, nearly statuesque in their discipline.

"At ease," King Marcellus said, raising a gentle hand. He strode to the table to pour himself a chalice. When Lord Valens made to serve it for him, the King gave a flick of his wrist. The exchange made Tollas beam with pride. It was astounding to see royalty swearing off the pampering of palace life. In the field, the patriarch of House Bethard had as much to lose as anyone, and such a simple gesture was enough to show that he, too, was just a man.

"Lord Valens," Marcellus called out after a sip of wine. "What word do you have of our negotiations?"

Tollas sighed, thankful he was not the one to break such news to the King. He stood silently and watched as Cedric reported the latest development, which Marcellus seemed unphased to hear. It was curious to witness how royal men conducted themselves. Even after receiving ill news, the King remained as calm and collected as a priest.

"That is disconcerting," King Marcellus said, stroking his chin. "But not unexpected. After all, that is why we are here, is it not? If the northern tribes were people of reason, they would see the benefits of accepting the Kingdom and its rule. Countless other tribes have done so since the days of my father, but these people seem averse to civilization."

"Sanbaen requests more time," Tollas blurted out. "But I believe he will accept. I saw the desperation in his eyes."

The King turned, their gazes locked. "Captain Noral. I would like to commend you for your efforts. I would ask you not to allow northern disposition to wound your pride. I have noted your good efforts."

"Thank you, Sire." Tollas bowed his head. To receive praise from the King himself was the highest of all compliments, one he would be forever honored to receive.

"Now, gentlemen," the King continued, "let us retire for the night. We must prepare our minds and bodies for what tomorrow may bring. Make sure the men are well-fed and rested."

Everyone inside the tent snapped to attention as King Marcellus departed, the purple cloaks trailing behind him. Lord Valens shot Tollas a stern glare, a soldier's understanding between them. With a nod, he dismissed himself from the tent, eager to steal a few hours of rest.

His accommodation was modest, as far as officers were concerned. A simple tent with a desk and chair, set on a finely-woven red carpet. A simple bed draped with plain white linens. An oil lantern sat beside a pen and parchment near a silver flagon of water. Hardly the trappings of privilege, as one might imagine.

Tollas laid his head down, though sleep was fleeting. For seemingly an hour, he stared at the canvas of his tent, counting specks of dirt. He sighed, his mind racing from the anticipation of what was to come. It was a frustrating feeling for a man able to sleep during a thunderstorm but not before a battle.

As he rolled from one side to another, he saw an orange glow of torchlight outside. Curious that so many were awake at such an hour, or perhaps the camp guard was maintaining their vigilant watch. Annoyed, Tollas rolled onto his other side, sighing deeply. After closing his eyes for a moment, the light grew brighter and seemed as if it was glowing outside his tent flap.

A scream rang out, then another, followed by a cascade of panic. Tollas shot from his bed, a wall of orange and yellow light flickering. He snatched up his sword and emerged, stepping into a scene from a hellish nightmare. Burning tents and burning men surrounded him, a fiery maelstrom of chaos and death if there ever was one.

What… what is happening? How could this be?

For a moment, Tollas' mind raced from one scenario to another. Could it have been an accident? Perhaps a drunken watchman toppled over a brazier and caused the fire? It could have been anything, anything but an attack. Sanbaen was a man near desperation. Surely he would not have orchestrated such a cowardly deed in the middle of the night?

"To arms, men!" a soldier cried out. "To arms, I say!"

In a daze, the Betanthian camp stumbled from its slumber to confront the terrors of the night. Tollas surged forward without armor, hoping to rally the courage of his countrymen. They were flocking to the northern end of the camp, though carnage was erupting from every direction.

A figure emerged from the shadows, nearly black as the night. Tollas caught a peal of light glinting off a length of steel, which raised and fell like a shooting star. Instinctively he parried the attack and answered with a frantic slash. The foeman lept back, revealing skin painted dark with mud and hair as wild as tall grass.

A Northman, no doubt, appearing as ghoulish as a pit demon. Snarling, the barbarian closed in again, swinging his arming sword with punishing strength. Tollas parried again but felt his bones rattling from the blow. Any more, and his arms might crumble like old driftwood.

The savage drove him backward, the onslaught intensifying with each strike. Fear cut through his heart, and if he did not prevail soon, steel would cut through him in kind. To his salvation, a Betanthian armsman entered the fray, driving his blade through the back of the savage until a bloodied tip erupted from his chest. Tollas sighed and nodded, thankful for the rescue.

"Captain," shouted the distraught soldier, "what do we do?!"

It was difficult to make sense of the situation, given the absence of any proper defense. Nevertheless, survival was the only objective until the Betanthians could drive the attacking horde from camp. Tollas doubled over, leaning on his sword, gasping for breath but finding none.

As he made to speak, a dancing ball of fire drew his attention. It flickered from behind a nearby tent, bobbing up and down as it moved from one end to another. Torchlight, he supposed, likely a Northman seeking to spread the fiery carnage even further. Tollas hefted his sword and hurried toward it, his footsteps as silent as a cat.

With his sword at the ready, he rounded the tent and saw a Northman standing a foot away, wide-eyed and frozen in place. Without hesitation, Tollas drove his blade into the savage's nose, piercing it effortlessly. Blood sprayed like a fountain as he wrenched his sword free, the barbarian corpse crumpling to the ground.

Screams and the clattering of steel rang out where he had left the frantic soldier. Hurriedly he raced back and saw the

Betanthian encircled by nearly a dozen men, each snarling and taunting their prey.

I can't leave him to die like this. What sort of man would I be if I diminished in the face of adversity?

After drawing a deep breath, he slogged forward, eager to greet death with steel in hand. Better to be slain with courage in one's heart instead of cowardice, he thought. As he prepared to charge into the melee, a sudden thundering of the earth gave pause to every man around.

Tollas turned and saw King Marcellus Bethard riding at the head of a dozen horsemen, the eagle standard of Betanthia flying along with them. It was the most awe-inspiring sight he had ever witnessed. The King was clad in his breastplate but devoid of gauntlets, grieves, mail, and helmet. But despite such vulnerability, he rode into the fray with unwavering bravery.

"Have courage, men! Do not flee!" Marcellus roared. "For Betanthia!"

The charge was enough to break the barbarian's resolve. They scattered like a flock of birds in every direction, knowing it was folly to face down cavalry. The King continued toward the gate, determined to bring the battle to a swift conclusion. After watching the riders fade from sight, Tollas found himself again. He turned to the relieved soldier, both men awestruck.

"Protect the King! Go now!" He gave the soldier a shove and set off in pursuit. Tollas raced after the King on legs that burned like hot coals, shouting encouragement along the way. Men poured buckets of water on wagons and crucial supplies, desperate to save what little they could.

A chaotic fury erupted from the darkness near the gate. Perhaps the fight had turned, and the Borjifans were seeking to retreat, he hoped. He saw faint outlines of horses and riders wheeling and dashing about, steel glinting with fire. The golden crown of Marcellus Bethard glowed like a harvest moon, a standard by which the Betanthians had rallied.

Exhausted yet determined, Tollas trudged ahead. He saw the King and his bodyguard slay Northman after Northman, gallantly holding back the onslaught at the gate. How it had been opened was a mystery, likely the work of a traitor or a clever infiltrator.

Tollas' eyes remained fixed on the King, who fought with legendary valor. He watched Marcellus dispatch a savage with a downward slash, cutting the man nearly in two. Just as the battle appeared over, another Northman sprang from the shadows, maul in hand, and swung with blinding speed at the King's head. The golden crown fell, along with the man wearing it.

And then, Tollas saw only darkness. Nearly as quickly as the carnage began, it subsided. Screams of desperation replaced the screams of battle. Men were shouting in panic, Betanthian men, just ahead of where the King had disappeared. Tollas felt a crushing weight of despair fall upon him as he sensed the worst.

"Bring water!" a soldier cried out.

"Fetch a surgeon at once!" another hollered.

Tollas raced onward, nearly throwing down his sword. Torchlight glowed ahead, flickering off the armor of dozens of men formed in a defensive circle. What they were protecting, he could only wonder, but the answer seemed all too obvious. As he approached, a Royal Guardsman stopped and challenged him.

"Come no further," the Guardsman cautioned, his weapon pointed, words tinged with emotion.

"What happened?" Tollas demanded. "I'm Captain Noral. Let me pass at once!"

Before either could act further, a half-score of men rushed past, carrying a body on a wooden plank. In the dim light, he saw King Marcellus, his head bloodied and nearly unrecognizable. Tollas felt his heart sink and almost stop entirely. Even though the attack was over and the battle won, Betanthia appeared to have suffered a grievous loss.

Frantically, he raced after the King as the Guardsman carried him inside a medical tent. At first, the purple cloaks violently denied entry to all, but upon seeing Tollas, they allowed him through. There was a flurry of activity around a wooden table, the King's body lying motionless atop its surface. Surgeons scrambled about frantically, desperate to halt the bleeding and save their monarch's life.

"Dishonorable beasts," Cedric Valens grunted as he entered the tent, his face dirtied from battle. "We extend the hand of peace, and this is how they return our kindness?"

It was difficult to comprehend how Sanbaen could have orchestrated such an attack, especially after pleading for a reprieve. Tollas saw the look of fear in the man's eyes, the fear of Betanthia and its armies' might. He had expected another round of negotiations come dawn, not the near death of his king.

"Do you think he will live?" Tollas asked softly. It was a question not even the wisest surgeon could answer.

"Hard to say," Cedric answered, then turned to face him. "Commandant Denison is dead; that much is certain. He died at the King's side, as true a death as any man could want. It falls to us now, Captain. The men will look to us for strength and leadership, even more so if he dies tonight."

Tollas felt his insides quivering as he looked upon the King. A thick hive of bandages was wrapped tightly around his head, a growing red splotch at its center. It was frustrating to be so powerless at a time like this. Before he could speak further, Lord Valens placed an arm around his shoulder and led him outside where they could speak privately. A congregation of men grew around the tent, each desperate to hear if the King would survive.

"I have a plan," Cedric said, glancing to his side. "Come morning, those savages will be expecting us to attack. We will present our army on the field and fix their gaze upon us. I want you and our cavalry to circle to the rear of the village and attack. When the barbarians realize what is happening, they will turn and flee to protect their homes and families. That is when I will run them down."

A solid plan, though Tollas was not without doubt. Sanbaen had proven untrustworthy and unpredictable, and the dawn might bring with it any number of treacheries. Still, despite his reservations, Tollas had come to trust and admire Lord Valens. Sacking an undefended village seemed dishonorable, but he supposed a simple distraction would suffice. No one would miss a few burned hovels, after all.

At dawn, Tollas rose from a brief rest and donned his armor. A dreary gray sky awaited, from which no sunlight had shone for days. Faint trails of smoke still lingered in the air, accented by a haunting chorus of pitiful screams and moans. He felt a great sadness welling within him, as well as a fiery and indescribable anger.

You must stay focused. The men need you now more than ever.

As planned, his detachment of cavalry assembled outside of camp. Most were present, though some familiar faces appeared absent. Their loss was felt by every man under his command, though none more so than him. But there was little time to mourn their brothers in arms. Every man knew their purpose that morning.

"This treachery will not go unpunished," Tollas said, his voice breaking. "We offered the hand of peace and cooperation, and this is how they repay our goodwill? Let not despair infect your hearts, men! Let us turn not to grief for our King, but to the sword and the spear instead!"

A fierceness began welling within the hearts of each man, good Betanthian soldiers through and through. While words were of little consolation for the tragedy they had suffered, they would serve to stoke their resolve well enough.

"A fine speech," Kavran said, coming alongside him. "Words seem to be serving us quite well as of late."

"I only pray it gives them courage," Tollas said. "What more can be asked?"

"We should have razed Borjifa when we had the chance and taken their chieftain away in chains." Kavran ground his teeth, emotion and anguish within him. "And now our king lies on his deathbed."

Many things should have happened, Tollas supposed, but fate had other desires. With Commandant Denison slain and Marcellus Bethard clinging to life, it now fell to himself and Lord Valens to see the campaign through. Swords would now have to accomplish what words could not.

"Come, Kavran, let us finish what we began here."

With Tollas in the lead, they rode far from camp to the south, carefully avoiding unfriendly eyes. They cut east, then north, navigating narrow trails through a dense forest of gnarled oaks and jutting pines, a rugged land that conspired against them at every turn. Gradually, the trees began to thin until a vast clearing lay before them.

Borjifa sat just ahead, thin trails of smoke from hundreds of hovels drifting lazily into the sky. It was an impressive village by barbarian standards, a village of stone and brick, elaborate estates, and tall towers. Tollas had expected little more than mud huts and pits of squalor, but Borjifa was quite the opposite. Flowering trees and shrubbery made the village seem almost picturesque, the fantastical dream realm one might witness in paintings.

Armed men patrolled the perimeter, though their numbers were few. Borjifa's might was likely on the field with Lord Valens, staring each other down at that very moment. Tollas knew what to do but became unsure of himself. Should he attack too early, it might spell disaster for himself and his men. Attack too late, and Lord Valens might become imperiled.

"Looks empty," Kavran observed.

"We underestimated them once," he grunted, "I refuse to do so again."

Patiently they waited, every second feeling like the passing of days. Anticipation was quickly turning to doubt, and doubt slowly turning to fear. Every time he thought to issue the command, he hesitated, knowing any miscalculation could result in their defeat.

But suddenly, a disturbance rippled across the field and into the tree line. It was a battle roar, many thousands trumpeting its defiant call. It was the sign he had been waiting for; the Borjifans were on the field. Instinctively, Tollas drew his sword and held it high, signaling the brave riders around him.

"To destiny, men!" he shouted. "For our people and our King, Marcellus Bethard!"

Tollas' horse exploded from the tree line with a sharp kick, nearly three hundred riders beside him. They raced across open ground as fast as their mounts would allow, the earth thundering beneath them. A handful of sentries outside the village took notice and hurriedly fled their posts.

Screams of terror echoed throughout the stone streets as the cavalrymen advanced unchallenged. Soon his riders were pouring into the village, putting the meager garrison to the sword. Tollas scanned the streets as the Borjifans attempted a hasty defense, but his men's retribution was swift. Barbarians were trampled and cut to ribbons before they knew what was upon them.

A savage emerged from behind a hovel, spear in hand and desperation on his face. He charged toward Tollas with reckless abandon but was slashed across the back by Kavran, who had entered the fray. Another warrior charged forward, but Tollas wheeled his horse about, staggering the man, then parrying a sword strike.

Steel clattered against steel until Tollas sank the tip of his blade into the man's shoulder. The savage gasped and then fell to the ground clutching a gushing wound. Onward he rode, surveying the carnage his men had unleashed. Blood ran thick between the stone cobbles like tiny rivers, pooling into dark, red puddles.

Just rewards for a night of betrayal, he supposed. Within minutes Borjifa would fall, and Lord Valens would be victorious on the field if everything went to plan. How quickly his optimism turned to horror as black smoke and orange flame leaped into the air. Dumbfounded, Tollas watched the blaze spread with frightening speed, blanketing the entire village in minutes.

What are they doing?!

Desperately, he raced through the streets, shouting orders to stand down. As he turned toward the village square, he spied a headless mother clutching the remains of her skewered child.

An old man lay close by; his stomach opened from end to end, entrails spilled forth. Nearby, a handful of his men dragged a woman by her hair into a hovel, her horrified screams echoing throughout the square.

Whether by grief for their king or hatred for the Northmen, Tollas' riders had descended into a pure animalistic rage. He sat mounted, overseeing the most unspeakable butchery he had ever witnessed. He could do nothing to quell the massacre and, in shame, turned away.

There is no honor in this. What have I done?

Suddenly, he paused as a sea of men crested over the horizon. They were Borjifans, fleeing the field of battle to save their families. Lord Valens and the army gave chase, cutting down Northman after Northman like stalks of wheat. The plan had gone perfectly, yet so terribly wrong.

Tollas Noral rode silently from the village, unable to face the horror his men had unleashed. As he retired to their camp, he paused, remorse welling in his eyes, and watched as Borjifa sank into flame, ruin, and madness.

CHAPTER ONE

Two Years Later

THE ROPE SNAPPED TAUT, A VISCOUS THRASHING AT ITS knotted end. It was the tenth hanging in two days, and only mid-week. So common was the sight that few locals turned out to bear witness. Tollas watched from horseback as the brigand slowly strangled, feeling indifference in his heart.

"When will it all end?" he thought out loud.

Despite his best efforts, the countryside surrounding Brimnora was smoldering. Scarcely a day had passed without a report of another pillaging or murder.

"Seems as if the whole world has gone mad," Barryn Kance muttered, his mount stirring beneath him.

"Truth be told, I have never felt more uncertain of myself than I have these last months," Tollas lamented. "From Captain to Commandant, I rose. Most men would do anything for such status, and I would do anything to be rid of it."

With a gentle tug of the reins, he departed the city square, Barryn, his deputy, keeping stride. Brimnora was as bleak as it was inhospitable. Weeks had seemingly passed since daylight pierced a thick veil of gray clouds above. Perhaps it was the cause of Tollas' souring mood, he supposed. If only it were so simple.

"There are troubling times," Barryn chimed in, "but you have kept the wolves at bay. This city would be nothing but ashes if not for your efforts. The people cry out for protection, and you have done just that!"

"And yet they clamor for my head just as fervently. Perhaps I might be the next one to swing from the gallows if this barbarism continues unabated."

Together they trotted down a road of rough cobbles, their horse's hooves clacking like carpenter's hammers. It was a dreary city of gray stone and weathered wood, one at the furthest edge of civilization. Hardly the place Tollas envisioned himself being, especially after a distinguished military career.

Sometimes, he looked at the golden signet on his finger and felt like an imposter. After all, King Marcellus rewarded him richly for his actions at Borjifa, but Tollas knew the truth. All the riches and titles bestowed upon him were for things he could not do, as opposed to what he had done. Had he been able to temper his men's bloodlust, that fateful day might have ended differently.

They arrived at Tollas' estate around midday, the usual gaggle of servants and dispatch riders going about their routines. A man in a thick, swirling brown cloak stood patiently beside the front door. He was short of stature, short of hair, and short of beard. Not an uncommon sight, and one he was all too happy to ignore. As he dismounted, the man approached, face drawn tight and hands wringing.

"Commandant Noral." The rider snapped to attention and offered a bow. "My name is Lieutenant Anagar, Sir. I bring news from—"

"News and more news," Tollas waved dismissively, then strode to the door. "Leave your report with my deputy. The only company I wish to entertain is that of my wine glass."

As he made to enter, the rider cleared his throat louder than one would perceive as polite. Tollas turned and lifted an eyebrow, unaccustomed to such boldness from a commoner.

"I beg your forgiveness, Commandant," Anagar said, trembling, "but Captain Martis himself sent me."

"Kavran!" he grinned for the first time in ages.

A name most familiar and a face not seen in months. Since his promotion to Captain of the city watch, Kavran had become utterly consumed with his duties. Tollas thought bestowing such a title onto his friend would allow for a life of privilege. The reality was anything but. With Brimnora teetering on the edge of chaos, there was seldom time to sleep, let alone socialize.

"Tell me," he continued, "what news from the good Captain?"

"He sent me to deliver this message. My condolences, Sir." Anagar's eyes fell to the damp, brown earth. He produced a letter of folded parchment, sealed with a stamp of red wax.

Tollas stared stupidly at the letter, uncertain if he wished to know its contents. At first, he wondered if it was word of another barbarian incursion. Such news would be more inconvenient than anything, given its increasing frequency. But something in Anagar's eyes said otherwise. Hesitantly, Tollas broke the wax seal and unfurled the dispatch.

"Commandant Noral," he read out loud. "It is with my deepest sympathy that I inform you of the death of… your… sister…"

At first, the words did not register. He had seen Lilian only two days prior at a grand dinner with Brimnora's nobility. She looked so elegant and full of life, her golden blonde hair adorned with a tiara of shimmering jewels. How could such a tragedy have befallen her?

"Tollas." Barryn pursed his lips. "I'm so sorry. I have no words."

"She was discovered this morning of the fifteenth, murdered…" Tollas paused, staring at the message in disbelief. "Murdered… in her… bed."

Instead of despair, seething anger welled within him. Someone had taken the life of his dear sister in cold blood, in her very home. It was the most unspeakable act one could imagine, perpetrated against his own flesh.

"Captain Martis is overseeing the matter personally," Anagar said, looking none too comfortable. "He is at your sister's estate, and—"

Before another word could be uttered, Tollas turned back to his horse, a look of savage determination seared into his eyes. Without waiting for a squire to assist, he mounted and took off at speed, leaving his estate behind in the blink of an eye. Not even Barryn's frantic shouts were enough to dissuade him.

Onward he raced across the breadth of Brimnora, a million panicked thoughts riding beside him, each jockeying for position in his heart. He felt a blistering hatred more scalding than a summer sun, and a deep sorrow so black and endless it could swallow the entirety of the earth and still not be sated. And numbness, so cold, bitter, and indifferent.

Each district within the city represented another era of its development. Tollas galloped through the market nearest the central square. He passed by weathered stone dwellings from when Brimnora was a barbarian settlement. While an eyesore against a growing backdrop of brick and marble, they were prized by Betanthian nobility as trophies from a bygone era.

Tollas saw little appeal in such things, even for the courtesies bestowed upon him as he rode. Not even the simpering of Brimnora's wealthiest could drive away the anguish in his heart. Street by street, the hovels and halls of old gave way to grand estates and enterprises, true Betanthian architecture if there ever was. Once the crowning achievement of his rule as Commandant, it all meant so little now.

The peaks of Lilian's estate appeared just ahead, jutting over the surrounding rooftops. A flutter took hold in Tollas' stomach, nearly sending him to retching. But as quickly as the feeling arrived, it departed, as he saw a detachment of city watchmen standing guard outside. At their head was Kavran Martis, the truest friend a man could ask for.

Despite having seen him only months prior, Kavran appeared to have aged a decade or more. It seemed the stress of his station had taken a considerable toll on an otherwise vigorous man. Silver strands streaked through his scruffy hair, framing a weary face that looked like an old saddle bag. At first, Tollas could hardly recognize him.

"It's good to see you, my friend," he said while dismounting, his mouth tightening into a frown.

"My condolences to you for your loss." Kavran gave him a quick embrace. "Nobody has been inside since I concluded my investigation."

Tollas studied the estate's facade, dreading to know the terrible events which transpired inside.

"How… how could such a thing have happened?" he asked, voice wavering.

"I wish I had answers for you. Truly, I do," Kavran sighed. "My heart breaks for you. Every day when the sun rises, I recognize this world a little less."

If one could even recognize it at all, Tollas thought. Still, his mind refused to accept what his eyes plainly read in ink. "Is she?" he asked hesitantly. "Still inside?"

"Yes, but I would advise against entering." An uneasiness crept across Kavran's face, most uncharacteristic of such a hardened man. "What was done to her… well… it would do you more harm than good to see her in such a state."

At first, Tollas felt offended, as if his friend's words were an insult. It seemed beyond comprehension that anyone could inflict such cruelties on someone like Lilian, the most gentle and charitable soul he had ever known. With a scoff, he pushed passed Kavran and made for the door.

"I beseech you, old friend, please," Kavran pleaded. "Don't go in there. My men have scoured the building for clues. There's nothing for you inside."

Part of him feared to enter; Kavran's expression was telling enough. In their decades-long friendship, he had never seen the man look anything but unshaken, even in the direst of circumstances.

"I have to see her," Tollas said softly. "I owe her that much. She's the only family I had left. And I know she would do the same for me."

Kavran sighed and nodded, then stepped aside. Tollas took hold of the door handle, a slight tremble betraying his otherwise iron grip. A rush of stale air greeted him as he entered. Despite familiar surroundings, something about Lilian's estate seemed so foreign.

An intruder had been here mere hours ago, befouling its once-welcoming aura. Although the area was secure, Tollas felt his hand drifting down to his arming sword. Each step made his heart race faster until the grand staircase appeared. Every instinct was screaming to turn back, but honor commanded otherwise.

As he climbed, Tollas' imagination began to run wild. Reaching the top, he could practically see visions of the mysterious intruder slinking down the hallway, steel in hand and evil intentions at heart. But despite a pang of protective instincts, nothing more could be done for poor Lilian. He approached his sister's bedroom; the door left ajar.

Lilian lay on the bed, a white sheet draped over her body. Dark, red splotches stained its once pristine fabric. Tollas sighed, struggling to contain the grief within him. Even in death, he had to remain strong for his sister.

"Oh my dearest…" he whispered, stepping delicately into the room. "I am so sorry. Never would I thought such a fate would befall you."

A macabre curiosity overcame him, the most unspeakable thoughts entering his mind. Something compelled Tollas to remove the sheet and witness the horrors that sweet Lilian had to suffer. The thought was first rejected but returned as quickly as it departed.

Forgive me, sister. But I must know what they have done to you. I have to see with my own eyes the pain you suffered.

With wavering courage, Tollas threw back the sheet, his eyes instantly slamming shut. Lilian was slaughtered like a pig. Hundreds of deep, bloody lacerations raked across her pale white flesh from face to feet. Her eyes and jaw were nearly removed, and a large, strange symbol was carved into her forehead.

Sighing and fighting the urge to vomit, Tollas looked again, studying the butcher's handiwork firsthand. How anyone could do such a thing to gentle Lilian was beyond imagination. Even the vilest murderers were dispatched by a headsman's axe or noose, a civilized end for uncivilized men.

Tollas stared long and hard at the symbol slashed into her forehead, pondering its meaning and wondering to whom it may belong. His fist began to clench tighter and tighter until it trembled uncontrollably. The villain responsible would soon come to regret their audacity.

"Whoever they are, wherever they are, they will beg for death before the end, my sister. This I swear to you. I will not rest until I tear their heart from their chest... just as mine has been torn out."

A quiver took hold in Tollas' lip as he placed the sheet delicately back over his sister's body.

"Sleep well now, Lilian. I will find whoever did this to you... whatever the cost may be."

He left the bedroom and shut the door slowly. A cleaning bucket sat outside a door just down the hall. Tollas staggered over to it and doubled over, his guts churning and twisting. A torrent of vomit erupted from his mouth, the sight and smell of Lilian's demise overpowering. After spitting a few times, he shambled downstairs and made for a bar on the far side of the parlor.

There, he poured a generous glass of brandy and gulped half of it down instantly. After refilling the glass, he slumped onto a comfortable high-back chair upholstered in fine velvet. Overcome by a deluge of despair and a rage so powerful it could split the earth, Tollas let loose a fiery scream. So loud was his cry that, perhaps, Lilian might hear it in the next life, and know she would soon be avenged.

CHAPTER TWO

IT WAS A LOVELY SERVICE, REPLETE WITH ALL THE SPLENDOR House Noral could afford. Thousands of flowers lined the freshly filled hole where Lilian lay, a simple wooden marker placed at its head. Tollas stood for an hour after the burial ended, reflecting on her life and his status as the last of his House.

Kavran and Barryn lingered nearby but were mindful to keep their distance. After all, one could not simply rush a final goodbye to a loved one. They approached only when Tollas turned away, garbed in his finest blue silks and a freshly-woven silver cloak.

"I have not the words to express how sorry I am," Kavran said, hands resting in front of him. "I swear to you, my brother, I will exhaust every effort to bring her killer to justice."

Tollas sighed, too exhausted to weep. He produced a small piece of parchment and handed it over. "Tell me, what do you know of this symbol?"

Kavran looked over the sketch but folded it after a mere second. Curious, as it appeared to be anything but foreign to him. Clearly, there was more behind its meaning than Tollas initially believed.

"I first saw it a month ago, maybe two." Kavran slipped the parchment into his pocket. "There was a raid at a homestead a few miles from here. Terrible event. The whole family was torn to pieces like the wolves got to them, you know? This symbol was painted on the wall with their blood."

"Good heavens," Barryn said, messing up his face.

A disturbing development indeed, one Tollas would have expected to be briefed on. Together, they walked away from Lilian's grave. "I have heard nothing of this. Do you care to explain why?"

"Forgive me, Tollas," Kavran sighed. "I thought it was simply a band of brigands marking their territory. I've seen it twice these past weeks, each at a different homestead near the border."

"Have you discovered any information from the men we've executed?" Tollas glanced over his shoulder in search of prying eyes or ears. "Surely, one of them must know something."

Kavran motioned to a stone bench nestled near a pair of tall arborvitae. Together they sat, stealing a moment to survey the cemetery's beauty. It was tranquil and beautiful, a fitting resting place for Lilian. "Truth be told, the men we've killed had nothing to do with the attacks."

It was the most shocking revelation, which nearly sent Tollas toppling to the ground. He shook his head incredulously, unable to believe what he was hearing.

"Nothing to do with the attacks?" he said in rising urgency and hostility. "How long were you intending to keep this information from me, Kavran? This entire time I thought we were making progress when, in fact, we are no closer to a solution than we—"

"Tollas, I'm sorry," Kavran blurted out. He produced a roll of parchment, secured with a thin leather band. As he unrolled it, a map appeared, drawn in colored ink. "But we had to show the people we're doing something about these attacks. Can you imagine the panic if everyone knew the countryside was burning and there wasn't a thing we could do about it? If executing a few common criminals keeps the people from losing their minds, then is it not for the best?"

Despite his anger, Tollas saw the logic behind such deception. Still, the explanation did little to quell his frustration. "This is disturbing to me, old friend." He ran a hand through the hair across his brow, which was growing moist with sweat. "So, what *do* we know?"

"Here are the locations of every attack we've suffered since they began." Kavran's finger moved across the map, stopping briefly at several small, black scratchings. "As you can see, it's concentrated along this stretch of the border, but no matter where we station our men, we can never prevent another attack from happening. It's as if the perpetrators are always a step ahead of us."

The map contained an assortment of markings, nearly ten from the looks of it. Tollas stared at them, eyes squinting and head cocked.

"Tell me," he said, scratching his chin. "Where was the location of the first event?"

"Here," Kavran responded, pointing to a homestead closest to Brimnora. "And here was the second. And so on."

Strange for an enemy to place their first attack closest to Betanthian troops. But a pattern emerged as Kavran's finger moved across the map. At least, when he was looking at the map properly. Tollas took hold of the parchment, studied it, then turned it upside down. With his index finger, he began tracing a symbol between the markings.

"Does this look familiar to you?" he asked with an ominous tone.

Kavran took the small drawing of the symbol Tollas had given him and stared at it dumbfoundedly. Both men moved their eyes across the top of the map until a blank section became the subject of their focus.

"Indeed it does," Kavran nodded. "And each attack has happened within three to five days of one another. The last one being… two days ago."

With hatred smoldering in his heart, Tollas stared one final time at Lilian's grave. He silently cursed his friend for withholding information, though such knowledge would have done little to change anything. Determination could find its way through even the best-kept defenses, and the men responsible for sacking Brimnora's countryside certainly had determination in abundance.

"Come, old friend," Tollas said, "We have much riding ahead of us, and time is growing short. Let's turn the tables on these villains and end this madness once and for all. We make for Fort Thorncrest."

"There isn't time," Kavran said with subtle desperation. "And besides, if we ride to the village with a host, we're likely to scare the barbarians away if they take notice. Then, we'll have no idea where they will strike next. I have sixty men ready to ride at your command. That should more than suffice."

It was a dangerous gamble, to be certain. But the more Tollas thought on it, the more sense it made. The villages which suffered attacks were small and undefended, easy pickings for even a dozen capable men.

"I agree," he said, "There is a time for caution and a time for decisiveness. For too long, we have sat idle while the countryside burns. These bandits think us weak, but their hubris will be their undoing. Barryn, I need you to remain here in my stead while I'm away."

"But... Commandant, surely you must need—" Barryn stammered.

"I understand your apprehension." Tollas placed a hand on his shoulder. "But there is no better man for the task than you. See to my affairs, and keep the spirits of the city folk high. I intend to return soon with these butchers in irons. Mark my words, Barryn. Justice is coming, and it will be swift."

That afternoon, Tollas met Kavran and his bodyguard at the northern gates of Brimnora. Sixty men sat armored and mounted, each a veteran of Betanthia's northern wilderness. Fewer numbers than he had hoped for, but time was growing shorter by the minute.

Besides, each one is worth ten of those unwashed tree dwellers.

With iron determination, Tollas put a boot into the side of his destrier and left the protective walls of Brimnora. With his men in tow, they ventured off into the realm of savage and uncivilized men to face the unknown and, if the fates were kind, return with Lilian's killer.

I will settle for nothing less, sweet sister. The fiend who murdered you will be swinging from a rope before the week is out. Mark my words.

CHAPTER THREE

"ARE YOU CERTAIN THIS IS WHERE THEY'LL ATTACK?" TOLLAS asked, scanning the none-too-impressive landscape.

Despite being under Betanthian authority, the village was every bit as barbarian as one might expect: hovels of wood and stone, dirt roads, and animals wandering about. Hardly the sort of place worth plundering, as there was unlikely to be even a single gold coin anywhere.

Rolling hills blanketed the landscape, rising and falling like ocean waves. Some of the hovels appeared to be built sideways against the steep inclines of glacial carvings throughout the forest. A most unique sight, and a far cry from the flat terrain of southern Betanthia.

"According to the map, this is it," Kavran replied, though himself uncertain.

The villagers took notice of the eagle standard beside them but paid little attention. Fear of Marcellus Bethard was a currency that could only buy so much in northern places. Even the sheer number of riders pouring into the village square made little difference.

Tollas sensed fear in the air, but not from his presence. It seemed as if a foul wind had swept across the village, infecting the people with nervous anticipation. Something was wrong, and everyone knew it, it seemed.

"Certainly appears like we're in the right place," Tollas said as he dismounted. "It almost seems as if they know something we don't."

"Well, we *do* know," Kavran grunted. "That's why we're here. I'll get the men situated. Time is in short supply if our suspicions are correct."

Another obvious scarcity was the lack of defensive structures around the village perimeter. There were no walls, palisades, towers, or trenches, nothing which might dissuade an attacking horde. Such was the case in outlying settlements near the border. Tollas shook his head as he studied the layout of various halls and hovels, gauging where an appropriate defense might be made.

"Commandant," a Sergeant said as he came alongside him. "I hate to be the bearer of bad news, but there is barely a sword or spear among these people. They're mostly farmers."

"Then it appears we're on our own, should we find ourselves in a fight," Tollas lamented. "Still, it's only proper for them to defend their homes and families. Find the strongest men and give them whatever weapons we can spare."

A strong wind began building in the north, rustling the branches of centuries-old pines. An ominous silence followed, so quiet not even the birds were chirping. Something most certainly was amiss. A sudden, sharp buzz pierced the air, followed by a deep thump. He turned and saw the Sergeant fall face-first onto the ground, an arrow shaft protruding from his back.

At first, Tollas stood dumbfounded, unable to move. Another man fell mere feet away as dozens of shrill whistling sounds rippled through the air. They had barely arrived and already found themselves under attack.

"To arms, men!" he roared, drawing his steel with lightning quickness. "To arms!"

Hastily the Betanthians assembled themselves, rapidly dismounting and standing beside their brothers with shields locked. Arrows continued to pour in like spring rain, so vast in number there seemed no end to them. Villagers scattered and scrambled for cover, but some were felled in their tracks.

Screams and panic rang out like bells, women and children wailing as fear overtook them. A flicker in the corner of Tollas' eye stole his attention, orange and white and fluttering as a windblown banner. Within seconds, the thatched roof of a hereby hovel became blanketed in fire, quickly jumping and spreading with terrifying speed.

More fires erupted throughout the village, followed by plumes of black smoke. Tollas felt his chest tightening, despite a ring of shields around him. Whoever was conducting the attack knew what they were doing.

"They're trapping us!" Kavran shouted.

But there was little more that could be done. Tollas knew retreating at a time like this would only ensure the destruction of his men. No, he thought, a stand had to be made. The monsters who had killed and pillaged at will had to be confronted.

"Hold fast, men!" he cried out, pacing throughout the defensive circle like a caged animal. "Let not fear poison your hearts!"

Suddenly, the treeline erupted like a swarm of hornets, men surging forth with ferocious speed. Deep howls and shrill battle cries echoed throughout the burning village, so loud and numerous it sounded as if the earth was splitting. Dozens of Northmen charged in, perhaps a hundred or more, their numbers seemingly insurmountable.

The barbarians were every bit as ghoulish as Tollas remembered. Many wore skulls and horns and adorned their armor with bones. While it provided little in the way of protection, their monstrous appearance was every bit a weapon as a sword or spear.

Another deluge of arrows rained in, striking down several brave Betanthians where they stood. Quickly they closed ranks as the savages collided violently with their shield wall, steel and wood rattling.

"Push! Push, damn you!" Tollas shouted, dismayed at the brute force of his northern foes.

He stepped forward and delivered a sword thrust to the neck of a barbarian, who stood nearly a head and a half taller than any of his soldiers. As the warrior fell, he saw rings of mail and plates of steel hidden beneath animal skins and bones. Not the armor of disorganized bandits, as one might expect to encounter.

One by one, gaps began to emerge in the shield circle. The savages were every bit as brutish as their appearance and seemed to overpower Tollas's men as if they were children. A mighty great axe shattered a Betanthian shield and the arm wielding it. A sword thrust pierced another soldier's face, his empty helmet tumbling to the ground.

But for every good man slain, Tollas responded in kind. As the shield circle grew smaller and tighter, an ever-increasing pile of barbarian bodies began littering the ground. Still, despite a valiant effort, the fight was against them. Tollas knew they would not be able to hold for long, his mind racing to craft some scheme that might be their salvation.

When all hope seemed lost, a mob of villagers charged into the fray. They wielded spears and scythes, crude farm weapons meant to till soil, not tear flesh. A fortunate reprieve if there ever was one, he thought.

Thank the fates. Say what you will about northern folk, but at least they will defend what's theirs.

They charged into the embattled barbarians with reckless abandon, swinging their makeshift weapons without regard for technique. But it mattered little, as their numbers were enough to invite doubt into the savage's hearts. Though some villagers were cut down effortlessly, their sheer tenacity proved effective.

"Here's our chance, men!" Tollas shouted, wheeling his sword in the air. "Push forward!"

Onward the Betanthians charged, roaring and cursing with righteous fury. With Tollas in the lead, they again clashed with the barbarians, staggering their broken formation. One by one, he cut them down with ease, as if shrouded from the Northmen's eyes. Tollas closed the distance on a nearby foeman, who turned and raised an arming sword to strike, but promptly fled the engagement upon seeing him.

Suddenly, a mighty horn blast cut through the carnage, drawing the barbarians away from the village as quickly as they arrived. They vanished into the smoke like ghosts in the night, an eerie silence falling over the killing ground. Tollas exhaled as if he had been holding his breath the entire time.

"Cowards," Kavran said, panting like a dog. "Of course, they tuck tail and flee when faced with anything more than an old woman with a broomstick!"

While victorious, their men paid a heavy price. Many survived, but nearly a third of his men lay dead or writhing on the ground in agony. Most of the wounded, it appeared, would not leave the village alive.

"I, for one, am thankful it's over," he huffed. "I'm not sure we could have stood for much longer."

"You look disappointed," Kavran observed. "Would you have preferred if we had lost?"

Tollas sheathed his sword. "Our victory was nearly as costly as a defeat. Even if we wanted to give chase and hunt these savages down, we have not the men to do so."

With the village still burning, the Betanthians gathered their wounded and retired from the killing ground. They could do little for the dead until the hellfire ran its course, but thankfully its spread appeared contained. Tollas stole a moment to search the corpses of their northern foes.

Some were well-armed and well-armored, far beyond what a mere barbarian could procure. He spied an arming sword clutched in the dead fingers of a Northman, its hilt ornate and blade immaculate. A curious weapon for a savage to wield, but quickly its origin became clear.

This is Betanthian steel.

Unsurprising, considering the pillaging inflicted upon the countryside in recent times. Still, it was an unwelcome reminder of how many good lives had been lost to the northern scourge. His hands clenched into fists as he looked upon the sword, wondering how many brothers had succumbed to its fearsome bite.

But then, he spied a small marking on the barbarian's throat. At first, Tollas thought it was merely a splash of blood, but curiosity convinced him otherwise. He bent down, pulled back the tunic beneath the warrior's armor, and saw the painted runic symbol that had come to haunt his dreams.

"Kavran!" he shouted, glancing over his shoulder. "Take a look at this."

Captain Martis sauntered over, his sour expression unchanged. The symbol only worsened his mounting fatigue, which reflected prominently in his eyes.

"I remember a time when being right made me feel good." Kavran sighed, then quickly turned away. "We should find shelter and tend to the wounded in case they return."

A solid precaution, indeed. Tollas retrieved the sword from his enemy's hand, for it was only fitting to return good Betanthian steel to its masters. He assisted in gathering what men remained and found sanctuary in a mead hall, its walls thick with massive stones. A long table at its center once held bountiful feasts, but now held his soldiers' slashed and battered bodies.

Those unharmed stood vigil, scanning the village for any sign of the barbarian horde. Villagers began returning in small numbers, some arriving to smoldering ruins, while others found themselves fortunate. Thankfully, most of the people were spared due to the presence of Tollas and his men. It was a bittersweet consolation for all he had lost.

Across the hall were casks of mead and ale, some already tapped. Kavran filled a pair of mugs and joined Tollas at a window overlooking the northern treeline. At first, he was hesitant to drink, not only to keep his wits sharp but also in apprehension of the taste. Mead was a strange drink, but thankfully, Kavran brought ale.

"You mustn't be so hard on yourself, old friend." Kavran sipped at his pint, a thin layer of foam lingering across his upper lip.

"It's never easy when you lose men, no matter the circumstance." He peered down at his ale but was unable to drink.

"Indeed, everything happened so quickly. If we had scattered, those savages would have picked us off with arrows or simply run us down one by one. You did the only sensible thing. We held firm, and we won."

Memories of the battle played out in Tollas' head as if he were watching from high in the clouds. It was an expertly planned attack, almost as if the barbarians had been awaiting their arrival. But despite the high level of coordination, a disturbing thought began nagging him with increasing intensity.

"You want to hear something mad?" Tollas asked, taking a small sip from his mug. "Even though it was chaos out there, I never once felt like I was truly in danger. Does that make any sense to you? There were moments when I could easily have been cut down, yet I almost appeared invisible to them."

Kavran cocked his head and shrugged. "Perhaps those gods the Northmen speak of are real after all. Or maybe it was just dumb luck. Who can say? But I do know this; there's a reason we survived. We have business to finish."

Perhaps it was fate after all. Lilian had been butchered unceremoniously in her bed, and the heavens cried out for justice. It must have been providence that spared him injury on the battlefield, he thought.

"I believe you're correct." Tollas downed the rest of his drink with a few mighty gulps. "Let us steal a few hours of rest. The men could certainly use it. And I suspect the barbarians won't get far after the thrashing we gave them."

Though it was still daytime, rest proved easy to find. Despite apprehension of a second assault, Tollas nodded off for an hour, maybe two. Exhaustion made his eyes heavy and arms weak, made all the worse when he awoke. Perhaps it would have been better to have not slept at all, he thought.

After rising and stretching his aching body, he gathered what men could be spared, less than three dozen in number. Some were tasked with remaining in the village to tend to the wounded and protect them from further attacks. A risk, for certain, but one worth taking.

After gathering provisions, Tollas and his men prepared to venture into the forest, still weary but determined as ever. Perhaps somewhere among the horde was the man responsible for murdering sweet Lilian, and he would not allow the perpetrator to escape, not when he was so close.

Kavran looked troubled or perhaps shaken from the ferocity of the battle. It was unusual to see him in such low spirits. Tollas came alongside him and placed a hand on his shoulder.

"Come, old friend, and be heartened," he said with a half-smile. "Now it's our turn to strike."

CHAPTER FOUR

THEY SET OUT FROM THE VILLAGE MID-MORNING, A THICK
haze of smoke shrouding the sun. Many locals turned out
to see his men off, thankful their dwellings were spared from
barbarian fire. At least, most of them were. Though some had
lost everything, all were grateful for the intervention of Tollas
and his soldiers.

Some offered to care for the wounded to express their grat-
itude. A kind gesture, and necessary, given the ferocity of the
battle. Tollas felt apprehension building in his heart as he looked
over his shoulder at the men beside him.

*Less than half of what I set out with, and ten times less than I
would like to have.*

Still, thirty or so Betanthians could move mountains if
properly motivated, and the hate burning in every man's eyes
appeared to be motivation enough. Cautiously they headed into
the forest on foot to not alert the barbarians to their presence.
With sword and shield at the ready, Tollas led the way down
worn deer paths, only recently disturbed by footprints.

"They couldn't have gone far," Kavran said, scanning the forest floor. "Not after the thrashing we gave them."

"Perhaps," he mumbled, "but we've been anything but fortunate so far. I would expect them to be fifty leagues from here by now, for all their courage."

"Well, I wouldn't be dismayed just yet." Kavran muscled his way forward, sword and shield raised and ready.

Tollas turned and threw a hand into the air, his men readying themselves in kind. Had some clue presented itself? Or perhaps an ambuscade had been discovered? He watched Kavran stalk forward through a cluster of ragged shrubs, then followed closely behind.

As he prepared to face the unknown, they happened upon the corpse of a Northman lying between two massive spruce trees. A cold, dead hand clutched at a deep wound raked across his gut, his arms and upper chest a mess of cuts and stabs. The last of his essence had poured out onto the earth hours prior, staining the soil red.

"I told you," Kavran said, lowering his sword. "I knew these savages wouldn't make it far."

"Indeed," Tollas sighed. "I expect we'll be seeing more of this. And if we're swift enough, we might discover their camp before they scurry off to whatever dung heap they emerged from. Come, let's pick up the pace."

Hours came and went, and with each passing mile, evidence of the Northmen became more abundant. Discarded weapons and armor littered the trail, and three more bodies lay dead where they fell. Yet despite their progress, Tollas feared they were no closer to discovering the remnants of the barbarian horde.

The afternoon grew late, and the sun began its long descent across a sky of patchwork clouds. Every mile they walked grew more anxiety-ridden than the last. A sudden snapping of tree branches made the patrol nearly jump from their skins, but the frantic scurrying of a nearby deer was relieving enough.

Tollas stole a moment to marvel at the thick, tall trunks of ancient pines, so tall and mighty they nearly blocked out the sun. A mat of yellow needles blanketed the forest floor, rendering the trail nearly invisible. Thankfully, the injured shuffling of dragging feet was enough to lead them onward.

The cathedral of pines soon diminished, a vast prairie with tall grasses and juvenile spruces stretching for a mile or more. He sighed, wondering if they would ever come across the barbarian raiders. While the tracks remained, they seemed to lead to an end they might never discover.

"How much further for today, Tollas?" Kavran asked, scratching at a bug bite on his neck.

"For another hour, I suppose," he replied, shrugging. "If the trail continues like this, we should return to the village. Who knows where those fiends might be hiding? And knowing northern treachery, it would not be beyond imagination for them to return and finish what they started."

"Indeed." Kavran nodded. "Our wounded would stand no chance if they were attacked again. You're right, old friend, and I can only imagine your frustration."

Life seemed to be an endless collection of frustrations that grew by the day. But despite it all, his duty was to Betanthia and the men serving beneath him.

"Personal vengeance will have to wait," he said. "I cannot risk the integrity of our borders, as much as it pains me to say. Lilian would not want me to act foolishly on her accord. If we don't happen upon them soon, then we will retire."

"I admire your discipline and dedication to others," Kavran said. "Were you a lesser man, you would never have led us this far only to turn back. Most would have chosen to press on, consequences be damned."

It was bittersweet to think justice had been eluded. But perhaps with time and diligence, the barbarians might be made to answer for their crimes. Perhaps, Lilian might be able to rest peacefully with her killer swinging from the end of a noose.

"The burden of leadership," he sighed. "I know not when this will all end, but it appears it will not be today. When we return, I intend to redouble our efforts to rout these savages out from—"

A sudden whoosh cut through the air, followed by a thump and a groan. Tollas turned and saw an arrow protruding from the side of a soldier, who doubled over and fell to the ground. Half a dozen more rained in before he realized what was happening.

"Ambush!" he screamed, raising his shield. "Get into formation!"

Before his men could cluster into a protective ring of shields, dozens of savages burst forth from the grasses and behind pine trees, near to a hundred or more. His soldiers were spread out and facing down more archers than he could count. They looked around frantically for escape but found Northmen at every turn.

"Lay down your weapons!" a voice called out, deep and rumbling. It seemed to echo from every direction, as if coming from the earth itself.

"Stand your ground!" Tollas roared, inching his way closer to Kavran.

It was impossible to hear anything over his heart, which pounded so heavily he felt it in his ears. Soldiers looked at him with pure terror, desperate to hear some command that might be their salvation. But Tollas could see no way out, neither through force of arms nor surrender.

As he stood, sword arm trembling, a figure emerged from behind a thick fir tree. Standing seven feet tall, it was the largest man Tollas had ever seen. He wore a suit of plate armor, nearly as black as an eclipse. His head was encased with a steel helmet shaped like a skull, its forehead and mandible accented with horns.

"Lay down your weapons, Betanthians, or this field will become your burial ground," the colossus said. "Do not doubt the sincerity of my resolve."

"To what end?" Tollas shouted, sweat dripping down his forehead. "I've never known a Northman to take prisoners. I would rather stand and fight and die with honor than be butchered like a pig!"

"Are you certain your men feel as you do, *Commandant*?" the armored barbarian said.

A sudden rush of panic made Tollas stagger. This was undoubtedly the mastermind behind the raids and Lilian's murder as well. By some cruel twist of fate, the justice he wished to serve had now become his undoing.

A soldier laid down his sword and shield and raised both hands in the air. He appeared frightened beyond measure, barely able to remain standing. A trio of barbarians advanced on him, setting the Betanthian down on his knees. Archers with nocked arrows looked on eagerly, ready to draw and loose at the first sign of treachery.

"Learn to recognize futility when you see it," the barbarian chieftain said, stepping forward. "Lay down your weapons, and by the gods, I will spare you the sword. You will not receive another warning."

Several more complied, throwing down their weapons and surrendering without a fight. Others stood fast, though their courage was wavering. Tollas knew he had no choice but to comply for the sake of his men, but honor demanded otherwise.

"I will not die on my knees nor be a prisoner for you to barter!" he roared defiantly. "If you fancy yourself a warrior, then face me, man to man!"

Tollas managed no more than a step before he felt the sting of cold steel against his throat. The razor-sharp edge dug into his flesh, a warm ooze of blood dripping down his neck. Reluctantly, he threw down his sword, not yet content to die. No, he thought, his men needed to live, and they needed their Commandant to ensure it.

Cautiously he turned, ever so slightly, to lay eyes on the man who might claim his head. To his shock and horror, the man holding the sword was not an unwashed barbarian. It was Kavran.

"What... what are you doing?" he stammered, unable to comprehend what he was seeing. "Kavran... why?"

"I'm sorry, Tollas. I do hope you forgive me for this, old friend."

A sudden, heavy thump against the back of Tollas's head dropped him to the ground. Millions of tiny, bright stars danced across his blurry eyes, spinning and fading in and out of black. He clasped a hand to his head, groaning and trying desperately to find his footing.

Standing beside Kavran were a pair of barbarians armed with cudgels. He reached out to his friend, a man once loyal like a brother. Tears of sorrow clouded his eyes, the betrayal cutting deeper than northern steel.

"P…please," he begged, "Kavran… please, don't… do this…"

Again the cudgel was brought down, this time across his forehead. A sharp crack rang out as his vision blurred and faded. The last thing Tollas saw was the barbarian in black armor, looming overhead like a storm cloud, a gauntleted hand reaching down to claim him.

CHAPTER FIVE

ARK WAS THE NIGHT AS TOLLAS CAME TO, A SPLITTING PAIN enough to shatter his skull. He groaned and nearly vomited, uncertain if he was alive or trapped in a terrible dream.

Where... where am I?

His eyes strained to open, the light of a massive bonfire near blinding. Where he was or how long he had been there was anyone's guess, but the ache in his joints suggested it was hours. As he made to step forward, irons around his wrists pulled tautly, digging into fresh wounds. A length of chain was coiled around the trunk of a tall pine, securing him firmly in place.

Dozens of men knelt before the fire as if at worship. As Tollas' vision returned, he saw they were his men, bound by their hands and feet. Surrounding them was a legion of spearmen, shirtless and painted across the face and chest with woad.

"He's awake," a Northman said, peering at him with disdain.

At first, Tollas thought he was in a dream, similar to the terrible nightmares he suffered over the years. But as the bonfire's heat licked at his face, he realized this was anything but a fantasy.

Desperately he tried to shake the iron bindings loose, but their grip was indomitable.

Six men stepped out from behind the fire, shrouded in dark, hooded cloaks. They stood silently beside the roaring blaze, the spearmen lowering their heads in reverence. The tallest stepped forward and removed his cloak, revealing the face of a man he had seen years ago.

"You?!" Tollas croaked.

It was a face he remembered well from the fields outside Borjifa before that fateful night. Bald and bearded, the seven-foot barbarian was a walking terror. Damien was his name, encased in black plate armor, a tattered crimson cape draped around his mighty shoulders.

"Good evening, Commandant," Damien said, his sabatons crunching as he drew closer. "Long have I planned and prayed, and waited for this moment. And now, before the sight of the gods, we face each other once again. Tonight, we commune with our honored ancestors. We pay homage to our blessed dead, to the men and women whose lives you extinguished."

A shaman appeared from the darkness, holding a bowl of burning incense. He approached the fire, blowing clouds of wispy smoke toward the heavens. He spoke in a guttural language, his words more beastly than human. The Northmen stood silent, their faces sullen. Another cloaked figure stepped forward and lowered his hood, his face barely visible in the light.

"May your people rest peacefully, knowing justice awaits," the man said. His brown hair was long, and his face bearded.

"You have my thanks, Einarr," Damien said, placing a hand on his shoulder. "Without you, this moment would never have arrived. You are the truest friend a man could hope to have."

"I must take my leave," Einarr said, "and my people as well. This moment belongs to you, and the last of your kinsmen. As fitting and just as it may be, this is not our way. We can take no part."

Tollas swallowed hard, wondering what horrors might await him. Every racing heartbeat made the gashes on his wrists ache and burn.

"I understand, my friend." Damien nodded. "This is not a night for the Nothanek, no. Your souls need not be stained with the business of Borjifa this night. Go, and we will meet again come the morrow."

Einarr and his kin retired from the grove, disappearing into the night. Damien's gaze turned to Tollas, endless anguish and seething hatred creeping across his hardened face. "Tonight, you will answer for the crimes committed against my people and the gods. I am the instrument of their justice, and I will see that justice is served."

"I have no quarrel with you or your people," Tollas said, perhaps foolishly. "I killed no innocents at Borjifa, only men who faced me in fair combat. We were at war! We grieved for our king, who you nearly killed that night when you raided our camp."

Damien ground his teeth, but his frame remained unbroken. Despite rage and despair in his eyes, the barbarian chieftain remained stoic. "Were it not for King Bethard's unquenchable thirst for conquest, my people would still live. But I will not bandy words with you this night, Commandant. The time for words has long since passed. Tonight is a night for vengeance. But first, I have another matter to conclude. Bring him forth!"

A pair of barbarians led a man forward by the arm, his head covered with a linen sack. He staggered and struggled to keep from falling, gasping and panting in abject fear. One of the Northmen brought him to a halt, then ripped the sack from his head. Tollas' heart sank as he saw Kavran, his dearest friend, now turned traitor.

"You bastard!" he roared, spitting in disdain. "How could you betray me like this? You were my brother, Kavran! We fought and bled together for years! We suffered and triumphed at each other's side! Why? Why?!"

"Damien!" Kavran called out, ignoring Tollas' cries. "I have done all you have commanded. I beseech you to hold true to your end of the bargain!"

A deathly silence fell over the grove. Damien stood motionless, his mind undoubtedly crafting some sinister scheme. "Indeed, you have. And you shall reap the fruits of your labor."

"Kavran! Kavran, look at me!" Tollas' voice shook and nearly broke. "What prize were you promised to betray your greatest friend? Why would you forsake your honor so easily?"

Kavran stared into his eyes, fighting back a tide of emotion. "He has my family, Tollas! I don't know how he found us. I don't know how he took them… but he did. And he promised they would be returned to me unharmed if I did as he said."

"If he wanted my head, why not take it while I slept? Why let our men die as well?"

There was something more; Tollas could sense it. Kavran chewed his lip, glancing nervously at the barbarian chieftain. For the first time, he saw tears in his friend's eyes. Truly, something evil had transpired for such a man to break.

"I'm sorry, so… so very sorry," Kavran wept. "He took my family weeks ago, more than a month, in fact. One night as I returned home, he was inside waiting for me, with a half-score of savages beside him. I thought I was surely going to die. He told me my family was taken, and what I had to do to save them, and so…"

Unable to face his shame, Kavran turned away. Never in a hundred lifetimes would Tollas have imagined seeing him in such a way. But then, a sickening sourness took hold in his gut, bubbling and churning.

"… and so," Kavran continued, "I agreed. I… I… came into your sister's home one night and… killed her, just as Damien commanded me to."

"You?!" Tollas gasped. "You killed Lilian?! You killed my sister?!"

"I did what was necessary to protect my wife and children! Your sister, the raids, everything… it was the only way to lure you out of Brimnora! If you had a family of your own, surely you would understand! Please, forgive me, old friend."

From the darkness came a half-dozen barbarians, surrounding a woman and two small children. They looked as frightened as deer, staring at the captured soldiers and raging bonfire in terror.

"Isabelle, no!" Kavran pleaded. "Damien, I have fulfilled my end of the agreement. Please, let my family go!"

The chieftain lifted his chin, staring back at him coldly. "Indeed you have, but your redemption is far from complete. The gods have witnessed your actions, Captain Martis. They see the blood forever stained on your hands. They cry out for justice for the Borjifan children you slaughtered! Now, you shall reap what you have sown in the blood of my people!"

"No, please!" Kavran sobbed. "I beg of you!"

Damien thrust a finger at the dancing flames. The Northmen hoisted both children off their feet and carried them, kicking and screaming, to the inferno. Kavran bolted toward his family, desperate to save them at any cost. He managed no more than a few steps before being struck with the shaft of a spear and dropped to the ground.

A horde of savages pounced on him, stomping and pounding with merciless anger. Tollas watched, an unfamiliar indifference filling his heart. It was strange to wish that Kavran would die, despite a friendship forged over years and the tribulations of countless battles. But now, knowing who had butchered sweet Lilian in her bed, he felt nothing.

"Damien!" Kavran begged, spitting out a mouthful of blood.

His pleas did nothing to dissuade the chieftain. Damien watched as both children were hurled into the fire, their bodies flailing and writhing. Shrill, haunting screams carried far throughout the grove.

Isabelle lunged forward, breaking free from her captor's grasp. A mother's instinct was a terrible thing to witness. She charged toward the flames but was stopped short, the intense heat keeping her at bay. Isabelle tried to rescue her children again but sank to her knees as their bodies grew still and voices silent. She looked at Kavran in utter hopelessness, eyes red and swollen from tears.

A Northman snatched up Isabelle, holding her as if she were a sack of flour. Tollas watched as she kicked and screamed and tried to break free. With a howling roar, the barbarian tossed her effortlessly into the flames, her gown igniting in a near instant. She thrashed and screamed so shrill it shook Tollas to his core. The stench of burning hair and melting flesh nearly made him retch.

"No! NOOOO!" Kavran wailed, beating his fists against the earth.

"You see, Betanthian?" Damien stepped forward, drawing a fearsome bastard sword. "Now, you have suffered as we have suffered. By the gods' will, your sins have come back to face you. And now, you will stand before them to atone!"

Damien raised his sword, light dancing off its viciously sharp edge, and brought it down with unrelenting force. Kavran raised an arm to shield himself, but it was cleaved in two, just below the elbow. He wailed in agony, clutching a bloody stump, legs kicking wildly. Again the sword was brought down, and yet again, until Tollas could no longer keep his eyes open.

A Northman took notice and delivered an unexpected fist to his jaw. His head was wrenched back and eyes peeled open, forced to look upon the butchered remains of his once best friend. Tollas felt nothing, a cold emptiness he had never experienced before. Lilian's killer was brought to justice, but not in the way he had imagined.

"Killing us won't bring them back," he said, though fearing it was unwise. "Not even an ocean of blood nor the world set ablaze could ever undo what was done."

Damien snarled like a beast, his blood-soaked face turning toward him. "You are correct, Betanthian. Our beloved dead rest in Sjenohor, where they await us upon our deaths. No gift of gold nor sacrifice of flesh could ever restore what you so viciously have taken from my people."

"Then let us be done with this before more families are destroyed. Let us part ways before more wives are widowed. You have the power to do this. I do not agree with what happened at Borjifa. I hung my head in shame for my part, though I tried to stop the madness before it consumed my men."

"You ask this, knowing it is impossible." Damien sunk the tip of his bastard sword into the ground, its blade effortlessly cleaving through the compacted earth. "What I do here tonight is not for those who were murdered, no. They are dead and do not care for the woes of the living. And while killing your men will never bring my people back, it is no less than you deserve."

One by one, soldiers were fed into the fire, its ravenous flames climbing higher with each victim it consumed. Tollas watched helplessly as his men begged for their lives, desperately trying to break their bindings and find an escape. For their efforts, they became fuel for Damien's terrible fire. It was the most shocking act of human cruelty one could imagine, unrivaled by any before it. Truly, it would be one of the darkest days in Betanthian history, if any survived to tell the tale.

Men flailed and begged, some weeping hysterically as they were dragged toward the flames. As the inferno consumed their bodies and grew low, another was fed into it, stoking its ferocity once again. A dense fog of burnt flesh was so nauseating that Tollas gagged and vomited.

Suddenly, a soldier slipped his restraints and sprinted frantically toward the treeline. The Northmen descended upon him like a pack of wolves, hacking and slashing limb from limb, taking their time with their butchery.

Hours passed until only Tollas remained. As the fire finally dwindled, it revealed a pile of charred skeletons. Each one belonged to a brave man, a man of king and country, now reduced to ash. He stared at their remains with utter hopelessness, his eyes misty and stinging from smoke.

From the waning darkness came three figures clustered together. As they drew close, Tollas saw two men carrying another, tall and thick as a mountain. He was shirtless and stumbling like a drunkard, chest wrapped tightly with wet, red bandages.

"Allarg!" Damien said in astonishment. "You should not be here, my friend. You must—"

"Silence!" the massive barbarian groaned. "My time is short. And I have come to see what we have accomplished here… all we planned and struggled to achieve these past two years."

"It will never be enough to bring our people back," Damien lamented, moving to Allarg's side. "But their spirits are with us tonight, as are the gods."

The wounded Northman wheezed, his eyes glassy and vacuous. He motioned gently with his hand, strength rapidly diminishing. "Come. Kneel before me."

Tollas watched with bated breath as Damien knelt and bowed his head in reverence. Allarg pushed the men beside him away, determined to stand under his own power.

"Many years ago… for my deeds on the battlefield… I was named Shieldbreaker. None…" he gasped, straining for breath, "none could stand before me; all fell to my axe's bite. My Soul Name shall live on forever, my deeds remembered by the gods… and our kin who survive. For your actions this night, for avenging our people, I name you as I was once named. May you be known by the gods and by your enemies as Damien… Dread… fire…"

Allarg nearly collapsed, blood erupting from his mouth. Quickly he was surrounded by Northmen and kept upright. He dabbed his finger on his blood-soaked bandages and slowly drew a runic symbol on Damien's forehead with a trembling hand. Seconds later, he lost consciousness and fell limp.

Damien stood and held Allarg's head in both hands, studying him briefly. "Thank you for bestowing such an honor upon me, my friend. I will not let our people down, nor allow their memory to be forgotten. Take him to the shamans at once."

Somberly, Shieldbreaker was carried from the field, the Northmen lowering their heads in kind. It was likely that Allarg was wounded in the battle at the village, and would never leave this place alive. Damien appeared disoriented, both at the mortality of his kinsman and from the honor he had received.

At first, Tollas thought he might have been forgotten, but Damien's cold gaze reminded him otherwise. The chieftain eyed him with growing rage, as another Borjifan appeared to have met his demise.

"Killing me won't change anything," Tollas croaked, his throat dry as sand. "And I'm not even the man responsible. I was only a Captain at the time. Lord Valens is who your quarrel lies with."

"Of this, you are correct," Damien said, drinking from a waterskin. "Cedric the Butcher will meet the gods soon enough, but all in good time."

"Then why?" he asked, trying to mask his desperation. "If it's Cedric you want, why kill my men? Why kill my sister? Why do any of this if he is the man you hate most?"

It made little sense to terrorize Brimnora when Lord Valens was hundreds of miles to the west. But a disturbing thought came to him as he looked into Damien's cold, black eyes. The warlord must have sensed it, as a wicked smile began creeping across his face.

"Because," Tollas said, answering his own question, "Cedric was always your true target. You came after me first so I could not assist him when you strike."

"How very astute of you," Damien chuckled. "And with Captain Martis in pieces, who will serve as northern Commandant? I am certain King Bethard will replace you soon enough, but when word of this night spreads, will they dare to intervene when I visit my wrath upon Lord Valens? I think not."

A calculated and unexpected move coming from a barbarian. Damien had proven the folly of assuming such people were simple-minded. He approached and removed the crimson cape from around his mighty shoulders, the fabric marred by rips and holes.

"This belonged to our chieftain, Sanbaen. He fell at Borjifa, cut down for the crime of protecting his people. And now, the responsibility falls to me to avenge him and the lives of every man and woman who died. Including my family... the ones I loved most in this world."

A sudden rush of fear made Tollas nearly black out. "I… I…"

"Let us speak no more," Damien interrupted, placing the cape back around his shoulders. "Our business has been concluded. Now, you will stand before the gods. And that, good Commandant, is a fate worse than death."

With lightning quickness, Damien wrenched his bastard sword from the earth and slashed Tollas' abdomen. The pain was so searing all he could do was gasp, his entrails spilling onto the earth. Terror-stricken, he watched as Damien wound up another blow and winced as the blade struck again. Silence and darkness claimed Tollas Noral as his head slipped from his shoulders and tumbled free.

Damien hawked his throat and spat on the remains. After sheathing his sword, he surveyed the macabre scene with bittersweet satisfaction. With his band of Northmen, they disappeared into the misty forest. A new day had dawned for Betanthia, but it was a day of blood, of hate, and of vengeance. It was a day that would never be forgotten. A day that would forever stain the pages of history red.

The Saga continues…

A WORD FROM THE AUTHOR

Thank you so much for taking the time to read *The Servitor of Sin*! Despite being only a novella, I found this story a challenge to write and finish. I truly hope you enjoyed it.

If you did, please leave a great review (or rating, at least) on Amazon or Barnes & Noble, as well as Goodreads. It only takes a few minutes, and it's the best way for you to support my work and get the word out. Doing so will help ensure that I will be able to continue publishing long into the future.

From the bottom of my heart, thank you for your fantastic support!

— *Chris*